THE ADVENTURES OF
MRS PEPPERPOT

THE ADVENTURES OF MRS PEPPERPOT

A RED FOX BOOK 978 1 849 41223 0

First published in Great Britain by Red Fox,
an imprint of Random House Children's Books

A Random House Group Company

This edition published 2010

Mrs Pepperpot Learns to Swim first published by Hutchinson, 2005
Mrs Pepperpot Minds the Baby first published by Hutchinson, 2005

1 3 5 7 9 10 8 6 4 2

Red Fox Books are published by Random House Children's Books,
61-63 Uxbridge Road, London W5 5SA

www.**kids**at**randomhouse**.co.uk
www.**rbooks**.co.uk

Addresses for companies within The Random House Group Limited can be found at:
www.randomhouse.co.uk/offices.htm

THE RANDOM HOUSE GROUP Limited Reg. No. 954009

A CIP catalogue record for this book is available from the British Library.

Printed in China

THE ADVENTURES OF
MRS PEPPERPOT

ALF PRØYSEN ❖ HILDA OFFEN

RED FOX

MRS PEPPERPOT
LEARNS TO SWIM

In the warm weather Mrs Pepperpot always walked through the wood when she went shopping. In the middle of the wood was a large pool where the village children swam. They splashed about and raced each other up and down.

Mrs Pepperpot always stopped to watch and she would sigh to herself and think, If only I could do that! Because nobody had taught her to swim when she was a little girl.

One day when she got home she decided to practise swimming in the kitchen. She balanced herself on her tummy on the kitchen stool but when she flung out her arms, she knocked a saucepan of soup off the stove!

Every night she would dream about swimming. One night she dreamed she could do the breaststroke. She stretched forward her arms, bent her knees and then – WHAM! – one foot almost kicked a hole in the wall, the other knocked Mr Pepperpot out of bed!

"What's the matter with you?" said Mr Pepperpot.

"I'm swimming," answered Mrs Pepperpot, who was still half in a dream, "and it's the most wonderful feeling!"

"Well, it's not wonderful for me, I can tell you!" said Mr Pepperpot crossly.

Then came a bright, warm day when all the village children were going on a picnic in the mountains.

That's good, thought Mrs Pepperpot. There'll be no children in the pool today and I'll have a chance to learn how to swim. And she walked through the wood to the pool.

It certainly looked inviting, with the sun shining down through the leaves and making pretty patterns on the still water.

She sat down on the soft grass and took off her shoes and stockings. Peering over the edge, she could see the water was very shallow so she stood up and said to herself, "All right, Mrs P, here goes!" And she jumped in.

But just at that moment, she SHRANK!

And now, of course, the pool seemed like an ocean to
the tiny Mrs Pepperpot. "Help, help!" she cried.
"Hold on!" said a deep, throaty voice from below.

And a large frog swam smoothly towards her. "You should NEVER jump in a pool if you don't have someone with you," he said. "Now get on my back." And he swam to a rock so Mrs Pepperpot could get her breath.

"You're a very good swimmer," said Mrs Pepperpot.

The frog puffed himself up importantly. "I'm the best swimming teacher in this pool," he said.

"D'you think you could teach *me* to swim?" asked Mrs Pepperpot.

"Of course. We'll begin right away, if you like. Frogs are very good at breaststroke. You climb on my back and watch what I do."

Mrs Pepperpot watched how the frog moved his arms and legs in time.

Then he found her a little piece of floating wood and told her to hang on. And she pushed along with her legs, just like the frog had done.

After a while she found herself swimming along without the piece of wood.

"Yippee!" she shouted with excitement.

But the frog, who had been swimming close to her all the time, came up behind her and lifted her onto his back. "That's enough for the moment," he said, and took her back to the rock for a rest.

Mrs Pepperpot was feeling so pleased with herself, she wanted to carry straight on and learn the crawl.

"Not so fast, my dear," the frog said. "You must keep practising breaststroke before you can do other things. But I'll get my tadpoles to give you a show of water acrobatics. How's that?"

"Wonderful!" said Mrs Pepperpot.

"Come on, children," he croaked. "I want you to show this lady all your best tricks."

First the tadpoles swam
to the top of the water...

then they dived
to the bottom...

then they wove in and out of the reeds in a beautiful pattern.

And then, like aeroplanes doing acrobatics, they rolled over and over and looped the loop.

The frog had puffed himself up so much
he was nearly bursting with pride.

Mrs Pepperpot was just standing up to cheer the tadpoles when she found herself rolling about in what seemed more like a large puddle than a deep pool; she had GROWN!

As she picked herself up and waded out of the water to the bank she could see no sign of the frog or the tadpoles so she hurried home.

A few days passed before Mrs Pepperpot got a chance to go back to the pool. But before she knew it she was swimming along and she felt very proud.

Then she saw that she was being followed. There was the frog and behind him were all the tadpoles! The frog came to the top of the water and gave a loud croak.

"Thanks, Mr Frog," said Mrs Pepperpot. "You're the best swimming teacher in the world!"

"I told you so!" said the frog.

And with an elegant kick of his back legs, he did a nose-dive down into the pool and all the tadpoles followed after.

Mrs Pepperpot
Minds the Baby

Let me tell you what happened the day Mrs Pepperpot was asked to mind the baby. She was tidying the house when suddenly there was a knock at the door.

In the porch stood her neighbour with her little boy on her arm. "Forgive me for knocking," she said. "You see, I simply have to go shopping in the town today. I can't take Roger and there's no one in the house to look after him."

"Oh, that's all right!" said Mrs Pepperpot. "I'll look after your little boy."

"You don't need to give him a meal," said the lady. "I've brought some apples for him, for when he starts sucking his fingers."

"Very well," said Mrs Pepperpot, and put the apples in a dish.

The lady said goodbye and Mrs Pepperpot set the baby down on the rug in the sitting room. Then she went out into the kitchen to fetch her broom to start sweeping up. At that very moment she SHRANK!

"Oh dear! Oh dear! Whatever shall I do?" she wailed, for of course now she was much smaller than the baby.

I must go and see what that little fellow is doing, she thought, as she climbed over the doorstep into the sitting room.

Not a moment too soon! For Roger had crawled right across the floor and was just about to pull the tablecloth off the table, together with a pot of jam, a loaf of bread and a big jug of coffee!

Mrs Pepperpot lost no time. She looked about her and pushed over a large silver cup which was standing on the floor, waiting to be polished. The cup made a booming noise as it fell so the baby turned round and started crawling towards it.

"That's right," said Mrs Pepperpot, "you play with that; at least you can't break it."

But Roger wasn't after the silver cup.

Gurgling, "Wan' dolly! Wan' dolly!" he made a bee-line for
Mrs Pepperpot, and before she could get away, he had
grabbed her by the waist!

He jogged her up and down, and every time Mrs Pepperpot kicked and wriggled to get free, he laughed, "'Ickle,'ickle!" for she was tickling his hand with her feet.

"Let go! Let go!" yelled Mrs Pepperpot.

But Roger was used to his daddy shouting, "Let's go!" when he threw him up in the air and caught him again.

So Roger shouted, "Leggo! Leggo!" and threw the little old woman up in the air with all the strength of his short arms.

Mrs Pepperpot went up and up – nearly to the ceiling!
Luckily she landed on the sofa, but she bounced over and
over before she could stop.

By the time she had caught her breath Roger had found a pot of ink and was trying to open it.

Mrs Pepperpot had to think very quickly indeed. "Careful!" she cried. Luckily she found a nut in the sofa and threw it at Roger, making him turn round.

He dropped the ink pot and started crawling towards the sofa. "Wan' dolly! Wan' dolly!" he gurgled.

And now they started a very funny game of
hide-and-seek — at least it was fun for Roger,
but not for poor old Mrs Pepperpot.

In the end she managed to climb onto the sideboard.
"Aha, you can't catch me now!" she said, feeling much safer.

But then the baby started back towards the ink pot.

"No, no, no!" shouted Mrs Pepperpot.

Roger took no notice. So she put her back against a flowerpot and gave it a push. It fell to the floor with a crash.

Straight away Roger left the ink pot for this new mess of earth and bits of broken flowerpot. He buried both his hands in it and started putting it in his mouth, gurgling, "Nice din-din!"

"No, no, no!" shouted Mrs Pepperpot once more. "Oh, whatever shall I do?"

Her eye caught the apples left by Roger's mother. One after the other she rolled them over the edge of the dish onto the floor.

Roger watched them roll, then he decided to chase them, forgetting his lovely meal of earth. Soon the apples were all over the floor and the baby was crawling happily from one to the other.

Then there was a knock on the door...

"Come in," said Mrs Pepperpot.

Roger's mother opened the door and came in, and there was Mrs Pepperpot as large as life again.

"Has he been naughty?" asked the lady.

"As good as gold," said Mrs Pepperpot. "We've had a high old time together, haven't we, Roger?" And she handed him back to his mother.

"I'll have to take you home now, Precious," said the lady.

But the little fellow began to cry. "Wan' dolly! Wan' dolly!" he sobbed.

"Want dolly?" said his mother. "But you didn't bring a dolly — you don't even have one at home."

She turned to Mrs Pepperpot. "I don't know what he means."

"Oh, children say so many things grown-ups don't understand," said Mrs Pepperpot, and waved goodbye to Roger and his mother.

Then she set about cleaning up her house.

More Red Fox books you might enjoy

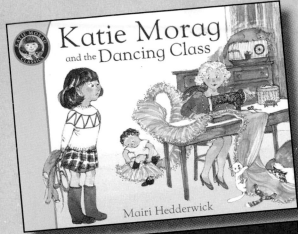

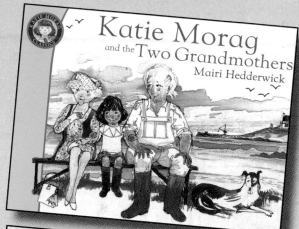

Katie Morag and the
Dancing Class

Katie Morag and the
Two Grandmothers

by Mairi Hedderwick

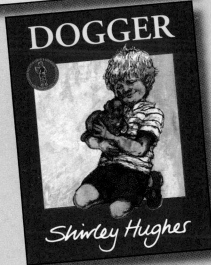

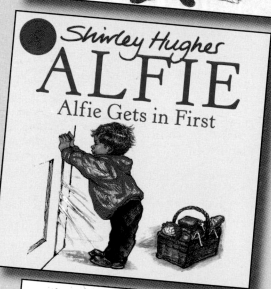

Dogger

Alfie Gets in First

by Shirley Hughes

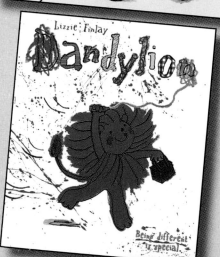

Dandylion

Little Croc's Purse

by Lizzie Finlay